Miami Jackson
Makes the Play

by Patricia & Fredrick McKissack
illustrated by Michael Chesworth

A STEPPING STONE BOOK™

Random House 🏠 New York

For MaJon, Star, and JohnJohn
—P.M. & F.M.

To #42
—M.C.

Originally published as *Miami Makes the Play* by Golden Books, an imprint of Random House Children's Books, a division of Random House, Inc., New York, in 2001.

Published in the United States by Random House Children's Books, a division of Random House, Inc., New York.

Random House and colophon are registered trademarks of Random House, Inc.

Visit us on the Web! www.randomhouse.com/kids

Educators and librarians, for a variety of teaching tools, visit us at www.randomhouse.com/teachers

The Library of Congress has cataloged the original edition of this work as follows:
McKissack, Pat.
Miami makes the play / by Patricia & Fredrick McKissack ; illustrated by Michael Chesworth.
   p.   cm. (A Stepping Stone book)
Summary: Miami's enjoyment of summer baseball camp is threatened by the presence of his nemesis, Destinee Tate, but for once he finds himself on her side.
ISBN 978-0-307-26505-0 (pbk.) — ISBN 978-0-307-46505-4 (lib. bdg.)
[1. Camps—Fiction. 2. Baseball—Fiction. 3. African Americans—Fiction.]
I. McKissack, Fredrick. II. Chesworth, Michael, ill. III. Title. IV. Series.
PZ7.M478693Mff 2004   [Fic]—dc22   2003017440

Printed in the United States of America

13 12

Contents

1
Here at Last

Monday, June 8, 8:30 A.M.

School's out. Vacation time, big time! All the waiting is over. We're here at last. Me, String, Horace, and Michael Keller—but everybody calls him We-the-People. We're all here at Camp Atwater.

Camp Atwater is a baseball camp. What a perfect place. Everything is laid out just the way the brochure shows it. Big lake. Cool lodges. Ten baseball diamonds. Yeah! What could possibly spoil two whole weeks of non-stop baseball?

Destinee Tate.

First person I see when I get off the bus this morning is Destinee Tate. "Well, if it isn't Mr. Know-Everything, Michael Andrew Jackson," she says, getting in a good word punch.

Nobody in the world calls me Michael Andrew. I've been Miami since my best friend, String, started calling me that when we were babies.

I cut back with, "So, if it isn't the Duchess of Much Mouth."

She goes over to the registration line. Can you believe it? Right away she starts whining about how girls aren't playing on the same team with the boys.

Well, duh!

Destinee Tate is the worst thing that's ever happened in my life, except maybe chicken pox or poison ivy. I've put up with her bossy mouth in class every year since kindergarten. This past spring, she started playing baseball—my favorite sport. That's bad enough, okay? But now she's followed me to Camp Atwater. Not okay.

9:20 A.M.

String and I just got our lodge assignment. We're heading over to Lodge #3 to check in.

I should be mad at String. It's all his fault that Destinee's here. He told her about this place. He talked it up, even had his mom speak to Destinee's mom about her coming.

String has been my friend since before kindergarten. But I wonder about him. He knows how I feel about Destinee. Yet, my best friend doesn't think my main enemy is all that bad. He says I need to get to know her better. I know enough.

"I can forgive you if you tell me that an alien took over your mind and made you tell Destinee about Camp Atwater," I say.

String shrugs as he takes his first bite of a juicy apple. Doesn't matter that he's just eaten breakfast. String loves food. "I told *everybody* who likes baseball about Camp Atwater," he says. "I also told We-the-People and Horace. That's how come they're here."

"What about Dracula? Did you tell him?"

"No," String says, looking surprised. "Does Dracula like baseball?" String flashes that smile that means he's not really serious. "Destinee's here, man. Get over it. Have fun."

9:30 A.M.

We find our lodge and meet Lincoln, our counselor. He's a junior at Tennessee State University, majoring in elementary education. He wants to start his own school one day. Lincoln has an easy way of moving, like he's got no place special to go. He's cool.

Lincoln shows us a map of the camp and points out the buildings. There's a main lodge where the campers meet and eat. He shows us the guest lodge, which is like a big hotel. Visitors will stay there on Family Weekend.

Lincoln points out the arts and crafts center, the swimming part of the lake, the stables, and a whole lot more. "You'll get a map and time to explore the place on your own," he says. I can hardly wait.

The camp is divided into sections—one for boys and one for girls—with ten lodges in each. The lodges are big log cabins with six bunk beds along the walls. All lodges have eleven campers who make up a baseball team and a counselor who is their coach.

So far, I like the guys we've been hooked up with. Most of us are nine and ten years old. Besides Horace and We-the-People, String and me, there's Allan Tubberman, from Madison, Wisconsin—answers to Tub. John Sparrow, a.k.a. Spare, represents Detroit. Billy Morris and Deshawn Edwards step up out of Chicago. Taylor Peterson has come riding in from Denver, and Kansas City gives us Jamaka Asim. That's ten. We're getting one more roommate.

Lincoln goes to turn in some papers. He tells us to unpack and get acquainted.

String and I flip a coin. I take bottom bunk. He gets top bunk. While we're all talking and finding out about each other, in comes our eleventh lodgemate. He's got red hair, green eyes, and a face full of freckles.

"Hey, man," I say, being friendly. All the guys introduce themselves.

"I'm Kenneth Peck from Atlanta and I'm eleven. I should be in a lodge with eleven-twelvers, but I registered late and they stuck me over here with you nine-tenners."

"Well, 'scuse me," says Tub, chuckling under his breath.

Kenneth flops his bag on the top bunk. This guy looks really tough—tough

enough to hit a ball to the far side of tomorrow.

"That's my bed," says Taylor. "There's a bottom bunk left over there under Lincoln."

"You take it," says Kenneth, scowling. "I want this one." Kenneth is big—taller than String even. Taylor backs down.

But String speaks right up. "Hey, wait. Keep your bed, Taylor."

Kenneth turns toward String. His red hair seems redder. His green eyes seem greener. And he looks at least ten feet tall. "Oh yeah? Who says?"

I close my eyes, not knowing what to expect.

"Hey man, chill," says String matter-of-factly. "Take my top bunk. I'll take the one over there. It's only a bed."

Looking at Kenneth, all I can say is, "Mission Control, we've got a problem."

11:45 A.M.

Lincoln comes back. He introduces himself to Kenneth.

"Look," says Kenneth, jamming his hands in his pockets. "Before we go any further, I didn't want to come here in the first place. Don't try to make me enjoy myself."

I'm thinking Kenneth is really asking for it. But Lincoln doesn't get on him for smart-mouthing. He speaks calmly. "Here at Camp Atwater you have lots of choices," he explains. Lincoln is really talking to all of us. "You can choose to have a good time or you can choose not to enjoy yourself. It'll be hard to do, though." Lincoln flashes a big smile. "'Cause there'll be so much fun going on around you."

I like that stuff Lincoln says about choices. I'm choosing to have a blast!

Noon

At lunch, here comes Destinee Tate. She starts to say something, but I hold up my hand. "Out of my way, Dust Breath." And before she can regroup, I'm heading for my table.

Suddenly, somebody slaps me on the back. "I like the way you slammed that girl," says Kenneth. "Way to go. We think alike!" He sits beside me.

"Wow, did you hear that?" I whisper to String, who's on my other side. "Kenneth thinks I'm ah-right." String doesn't answer. He's wolfing down beef stew.

After we eat, the head of the camp comes to the center of the room. He introduces himself as Robert Riverson, a former major-league umpire. He was also a very successful businessman who used his money to start this baseball camp ten years ago.

"You can call me Sandy," he says, taking off his Yankees baseball cap. "Everybody calls me Sandy, because my hair, when I had some, was sandy brown." We're all laughing, because he has more freckles than hair.

Sandy tells us what to expect over the next two weeks. "You came here to have fun, play baseball. Are you ready?"

"Yeah!" we all yell.

"Great! You and your lodgemates make up a team." Sandy is so excited, he makes us feel excited. But when I look at Kenneth, he's leaning back with his arms folded. He really doesn't want to be here. I can't imagine why not.

"Each team will practice together, learn together, compete together, and hopefully become good friends," Sandy continues. "We'll post your stats every day and at the end of the session, you'll get to vote for players on the boys' all-star team and the girls' all-star team. They will play our archrivals, the Lazy B Baseball Camp."

Sandy explains that in ten years, Atwater has never beaten the Lazy B teams. "But this year we're going to break the cycle," he says. "Bring home the trophies—one for the boys and one for the girls." Sandy really wants to win.

Across the room, I see someone waving

her hand like a flag. Destinee Tate. Sandy acknowledges her. Oh, man. She stands up. "Why don't girls and boys play on the same all-star team?"

You can hear a pin fall on cotton.

"That's the girl who was in your face, isn't it?" Kenneth whispers to me in a not-so-soft voice.

"Yes. Destinee Tate. We go to school together."

"She reminds me of a girl back home in Atlanta. I think I'm going to hate Destinee Tate."

"Really?" I say. I'm not sure what to think about somebody *else* hating Destinee Tate.

Meanwhile, Sandy clears his throat. "Destinee, we've never played boys and girls on the same team before. We won't this year, either." He tries to change the subject, but Destinee won't leave it alone.

"Why?" she asks. "That's so, like, yesterday."

"It's camp policy," Sandy answers stiffly.

Destinee wants to say more, but her counselor makes her sit down. Thank you.

1:45 P.M.

Soon as lunch is over, we head to our lodge. Kenneth asks me to walk with him—none of the other guys, just me. Cool.

Lincoln says we're going to choose a team name and colors. At first nobody makes a sound—not wanting to look like eager beavers. Lincoln writes down a name. "I've got a suggestion." He shows us. "How about the Pink Dragons?"

We're all looking at each other, almost in shock. "No way!" We-the-People says.

"I'm not playing on a team named the Pink-nothing," says Kenneth, arms folded.

"Thought you weren't going to play at all," Deshawn says, choking back a laugh. Kenneth ignores him.

"What about the Hard-Hitting Big Guys?" Tub puts in.

"That's silly," says Kenneth. But Lincoln writes down the name anyway.

"It does sound like a rock group," says Spare. "I like the Summer Bats."

Kenneth gives me a look that deliberately makes me laugh. Spare thinks I'm laughing at him.

Lincoln turns to Kenneth. "Do you have an idea?" he asks.

"Not really."

Lincoln moves on. "Any ideas for a team name, Jamaka?"

"What about the Monarchs, like from the old Negro Baseball League?"

Somebody else puts in, "The Beavers."

"I like the Eagles," says Billy.

Then I have a thought. "What about the Atwater Pikes?"

Lincoln smiles. "Nice idea, Miami."

"What's a pike?" Kenneth asks.

"A fish," says Lincoln. "A hard-fighting game fish."

"I learned about pikes from my father. He takes me fishing all the time," I explain.

Kenneth leans back on his elbows. "Your dad takes you fishing? My dad's always too busy."

Nobody says anything. Nobody knows

what to say. "I like the sound of the Atwater Pikes," says String.

Lincoln calls for a vote. He takes a quick count.

Tub suggests that since water is blue and fish are silver, our colors should be blue and silver. There's another vote. "It's unanimous," says Lincoln. "The blue and silver Atwater Pikes wins by a landslide."

There's that word again—unanimous. Unanimous is the word I missed in the spelling bee a few weeks back—put in too many n's. And Destinee won four tickets to a Cardinals game. Hard as I try, I can't get Destinee Tate out of my life.

Anyway, I like our name. The blue and silver Atwater Pikes. Sounds like a group of winners to me.

2
Losers!

Tuesday, June 9, 3:00 P.M.

Wrong!

The Atwater Pikes are anything but winners. We're here two days, practicing together, learning each other's moves. And making errors—plenty of them.

To look at Tub, you'd think he could really whack a ball. But no. He can't seem to connect. Poor Taylor is just as bad. Billy, Spare, and Deshawn talk a good game, but they're pitiful. Horace and We-the-People are a little better, but they're not all that good.

Kenneth turns out to be a really good

pitcher and hitter—maybe even better than String. But most of all Kenneth knows everything in the world about baseball. He's a walking stat book. Ask him a question and he's got the answer.

"We're on a team with a bunch of losers," he tells String and me on the way to the lake. "You're the only two who know how to play."

String climbs the high dive ladder. I'm right behind him. "Maybe we just need time to gel," String says. He steps out onto the platform and strikes a pose. He looks like one of those "before" pictures in the weight-building ads—or something. "The more we practice together, the better we'll get."

"How many practices do we have to have for somebody to just hit a ball?"

Kenneth argues. "You saw Jamaka drop that pop-up this morning? The few times we get on base it's from walks and errors. And what about Tub stumbling over third base and losing the chance to score?"

"So...? I don't know about you, but I'm having a good time." Then String grabs his knees and leaps, shouting, "Timber!" He swims over to the shallows where Destinee is dog-paddling around.

Kenneth and I make our leaps. But he swims in the opposite direction. He beckons for me to follow him.

"Is he always that way?" Kenneth asks.

"Who? String? He's always laid-back," I say.

"You call it laid-back. I call it two times squared."

I don't know what to say. String and I

have been friends forever. We're like brothers.

"But you, Miami," Kenneth adds, getting out of the water. He doesn't have a towel, so he takes mine. "You're okay," he says. "And since I've got to be here, we might as well hang out together."

"Sounds cool to me."

We touch fists.

I hear String calling me, but Kenneth says it's time to go. So I go.

7:00 P.M.

We've all gathered to talk about the activities that are coming up.

Sandy is saying, "You can choose a boat ride, a horseback ride, or an archaeological dig. You can sleep over at Clear Lake or take part in an archery tournament."

We get to choose two activities. I'm so excited. I'm going on the horseback ride and the archaeological dig. String chooses the same two without even comparing.

"What are you signing up to do?" I ask Kenneth.

"Nothing," he says flatly.

"Aren't you scared you'll get in trouble?" I wish I had nerve like that.

"Adults always say we kids can make choices. Well, let's just see."

Kenneth goes to tell Lincoln that his choice is to make no choice.

No sooner is he gone than here comes Destinee Tate. "Who's the wanna-be thug?" She points to Kenneth.

"Kenneth Peck. He's my cool, new, older friend," I say, feeling proud.

"Where's String?"

"Over there."

"That's strange," she says, "you two not being side by side. 'Cause you got a new friend doesn't mean you have to forget the old ones."

I shrug my shoulders. "Out of my face, Pickle Nose."

She waves me off. Then she changes the subject. "Hey, look, Miami. I think that girls and boys should play on the same all-star team. What's the point of having two? Would you help us get a petition started?"

Before I can answer, Kenneth is back. He's standing behind us. "No," he answers. "Girls don't know nothing. I bet you don't even know the first team to win the World Series in a sweep."

Without skipping a beat, Destinee

comes back with, "Chicago over Detroit, 4-0, 1907."

"So what? You memorized some stats. Bet you can't hit. Scared you'll break a fingernail."

"See you on the diamond, buddy."

"Me and Miami aren't helping you and no other girls play baseball."

Destinee looks at Kenneth. Then she looks at me. "Since when did you lose your tongue, Miami?"

What's that supposed to mean? Before I can ask, she's gone.

3
Impressive

Wednesday, June 10, 1:45 P.M.

Lodge #3 had kitchen duty at breakfast. The rest of the morning went the way it always does—a choice of crafts and a practice session before lunch.

Lunch is over. We're having quiet time back at the lodge. Kenneth and I come in. We find Lincoln taking a close-up look at the family picture I've got hanging over my bed. Lincoln smiles, trying not to look caught. "Nice-looking family," he says. "Your mother? Your sister?"

I nod. "The pretty one is my mother. The weird-looking one is my sister, Leesie."

"They are really pretty—your mother…
and especially your sister. Of course, you
are all—I mean—your whole family looks
good. You know what I mean?"

Lincoln is ah-right. I really like him.
But if he thinks Leesie is pretty, then
maybe he's not so bright.

Now we're heading to the diamond for
some much-needed practice.

2:45 P.M.

We're having our afternoon practice
game against the Crimson Bats. Kenneth
is pitching, String is catching, and I'm at
first base. The umps are always counselors
working with campers. There's a camper
and counselor at the plate, on the first-
base line, and on the third-base line.

Today, David is at the plate. He's as

round as he is tall with hair perfectly braided in cornrows. Best of all, he's good. Fair, too. I don't know the camper who is behind the plate with him. Lincoln is calling him Asher.

Nothing special about Asher—just an average-looking ten or eleven year old, with brown hair. He's wearing sunglasses so I can't see his eyes. Tub whispers to me that Asher is Sandy's nephew. Just arrived.

Asher's calling the pitches. "High, inside. Ball one," he says. David backs him up.

Kenneth goes into the stretch. He steps out and releases a fastball straight down the middle. "Strike one," calls Asher.

I'm watching Kenneth's technique. Boy, is he good. He winds up and sends another pitch blazing, a little to the left of the plate and low.

"Low and inside," says Asher. Holding up two fingers on his left hand, he shouts, "Ball two."

Asher calls the next pitch a ball and the next one, too. "Batter walks," he says.

Kenneth is not happy with the call. He jogs toward home plate, yelling, "What's the matter? Are you blind or something? That was a perfect strike."

David is laughing. Lincoln is laughing, too. They all seem to know something we don't. Kenneth doesn't get it. Me neither.

Then Asher lets Kenneth have it. "As a matter of fact I am blind, and I say it was a high, outside ball."

Blind? No way. Asher's accuracy is better than most umpires with 20/20 vision. And he can't see?

"I don't believe it," Kenneth says, waving his hands in front of Asher's eyes. It *is* hard to believe, but it's true. Wow! A blind umpire. It's sorta funny.

Suddenly, a big Lab that's been snoozing under a bench comes over and nudges her nose in Asher's hand to let him know she is by his side.

"Is that an attack dog?" Kenneth asks, stepping away.

"Hey, no. She's my Seeing Eye dog. She's been with me all my life, 'cause I've been blind all my life," Asher answers.

"But...but you called the pitches so..."

"The word is *accurately*. You can say it," David says, laughing so hard his stomach bounces up and down.

"How does he do it?" I ask Lincoln softly.

"It's a gift he has," Lincoln answers. "A great gift. Asher's got quite a sense of humor. I hope you get to know him."

Kenneth slams the ball to the ground and goes to sit on the bench. "Hey, come on," I call to him. But he refuses to play.

"Baseball is serious business. You don't see women playing in the majors. And you don't see blind umpires in the majors. So, no, I don't want to be part of some carnival freak show act," he says, just loud enough for Asher to hear.

"This aine the majors," I say. "This is Camp Atwater."

"I thought you were my friend," he says, almost whining.

"I am, man, but…"

"But what?"

"Nothing. Nothing at all."

7:15 P.M.

We're at the stables, ready for the late evening horseback ride. It's the first time String and I have been together since I hooked up with Kenneth. Asher is coming along with us.

We introduce ourselves. "I'm sorry for the way Kenneth, our lodgemate, acted today," says String.

Asher nods as he climbs up on a big chestnut mare. She's a beauty named Isis. I'm on a spotted horse named Paint. String's on a black horse with a white dot on her forehead named Pepper. All the horses are trained to walk. No matter how hard you try to get them to run, they just clip-clop along.

Asher's dog falls in alongside his horse. "Real impressive," String says.

"Impressive—like freak show? Or impressive—like a good thing?" he asks.

"Impressive as in *your dog is together*," String answers. "Your dog is real impressive." String loves animals. Always has.

Asher laughs. "Good answer. Good answer. You are so right," he says. "Juno is a star. I'm fortunate to have her."

In a little while Asher gets comfortable with String and me, and we're talking like we've been friends all our lives. And he's older than we are, too.

Asher is twelve. He's from Minneapolis and he's been coming to Atwater since his uncle opened it. I'm thinking the only thing to beat having a sports camp in the family is to live over an ice cream store.

"Without sight to gather information," he says, "I use my other senses." Asher pauses and tilts his head to the side as if he's listening. "No, Miami," he says. "That is not why my ears, mouth, and nose are so large."

"Can you read minds, too?" I ask. Asher's got a sense of humor that makes people feel comfortable with him—not always thinking that he's blind.

He goes on to explain that his ability to call strikes and balls is due to his hearing. "I hear the ball coming and by the way it sounds I can measure if it's high, low, inside, outside, or right over the plate. There's no magic or freakiness about it."

I'm all the time trying to figure out how Asher really—really—does it. He makes it sound easy, but I know it's not.

We spend the next few hours talking about everything from school to monsters.

Asher loves sci-fi movies as much as I do.

"You get to see the monster," he says. "But I get to imagine it, and I've got quite an imagination."

The horseback ride ends almost too soon. String and I are talking and laughing as we walk back to the lodge. Kenneth is sitting on the steps. He doesn't look happy.

"We had a ball. You should have come along," I say to him. "What'd you do all evening?"

"Nothing."

"Your choice," I say.

"This place is so boring!"

I want to say *no it isn't*, but I just go inside and get ready for bed.

4
The Headless Frenchman

Thursday, June 11, 9:45 P.M.

I've been noticing something. When I spend time with Kenneth, we do nothing. But when I do things with String and Asher, we have the best time ever.

I finally convinced Kenneth to come to the marshmallow roast and storytelling.

Sandy tells us a story about a soldier who lost his head at Frenchman's Bluff. Spooky!

"Every full moon the headless Frenchman comes looking for his head," Sandy says in a low, scary voice. "And when he doesn't find his head, he takes the head of the first person he sees!" And then Sandy lets out this blood-curdling laugh that chills our bones.

Walking back to the lodge, I'm realizing that the woods are dark. DARK! Darker than my closet—darker than underneath my bed—darker than the far corner of our basement. Anything could be hiding in the darkness. I have never seen dark this dark.

Lincoln walks ahead of us and reaches the lodge first.

We-the-People, Horace, Tub, Billy, Taylor, and Spare are all huddled together. Suddenly there's a noise in the brush.

"What's that?" says Kenneth. He sounds really scared. I'm scared, too, but I try to stay cool.

The noise comes again. This time it's

louder. Our cabin is just through a clump of trees.

Footsteps. "Oh, no," cries Lincoln, "not you again!"

String shouts. "The Frenchman's got Lincoln! We've got to help him."

"Not me," says Kenneth, hiding behind a tree.

"Stop, String! The ghost will get you!" I shout. But it's too late. String has taken off. I'm right behind him. Now all of us are shouting and running toward Lincoln.

"I'll save you," Tub yells, stumbling behind us. Our flashlights slice into the darkness just in time to see a family of raccoons scampering away with the goodies they had managed to steal from the trash can.

We pile on top of Lincoln, all of us try-

ing to save him from a family of raccoons.

"I wasn't really scared," says Kenneth. Yeah sure, I'm thinking. "All that stuff about a headless Frenchman is dumb," he adds.

"Sure was fun to me," says Jamaka.

We all agree.

The next morning, 8:00 A.M.

Stories travel fast at camp. At flag raising time, here comes Destinee Tate to rub it in. "Hear you led a charge against the headless horseman, Ichabod Crane," she says to String.

String admits he was terrified. I don't understand how he can 'fess up to being scared like that. He knows how Destinee is. She'll think of some way to torment you all the days of your life, just like Michael

Keller—We-the-People. She's the one who gave him his nickname—all because he confused *The Pledge of Allegiance* with the preamble to the Constitution.

But nicknames are not what's on Destinee's mind this morning. She sides up to String. "A group of us girls have started a petition. If we can get enough people to sign it, Sandy might let girls and boys play on the same team. Can I count on you?"

String shrugs. "Sure."

I don't answer.

"Take a look at the girls' stats. We're just as good as some of you boys."

"You got no competition," I put in.

"Are you saying no," Destinee says with her hands on her hips, "or should I ask Kenneth?"

"I don't need Kenneth to tell me what to do."

"Could'a fooled me," she says, strutting away in a huff.

1:15 P.M.

We just found out that Billy has a bad case of poison ivy. What is more miserable than that? He makes me itch looking at him scratching.

His parents have driven up from Chicago to take him home. We're all feeling bad. But we exchange addresses and promise to e-mail him when we get home. We'll miss him at third base, even though Billy couldn't catch a ball if it went down his shirt.

Billy isn't out of the camp yet, when Lincoln tells us that we're getting a new lodgemate. "Asher is going to join us."

Before we can say anything, Kenneth yells out, "The blind boy? Just my luck to get stuck with a bunch of losers and now a blind kid."

He doesn't see Asher standing in the doorway.

Asher is not into feeling sorry for himself. But he's got feelings. What Kenneth said is plain mean. I want to tell him so, but don't. None of us do.

Kenneth pushes past us and leaves the lodge. Lincoln goes after him for one of those one-on-one talks that never work with Kenneth.

Asher turns to leave without saying anything. Jamaka calls him back. "Kenneth doesn't speak for us," he says. "Does he?"

Everybody is looking at me.

What?

"It was really Billy's idea that I move in," says Asher. "I went to see him at the infirmary and he suggested it to Lincoln. I guess I should have asked you guys if you wanted me."

"Stay with us. Stay with us."

The voices stop and everybody is still. Juno's tail is flip-flopping from side to side on the wooden floor. We wait for his answer. "Well, Juno seems happy here. I will be, too."

Lincoln and Kenneth come back in. Although Kenneth apologizes to Asher, it doesn't sound real. Kenneth can be so much fun sometimes—when we're playing a game or talking baseball stats. And I'm proud to be his friend. But, at times like this, he's a real jerk.

5
A Choice to Lose

Saturday, June 13, 4:30 P.M.

Word's spread that David is letting Asher ump a real game with a girl. It's a first for both.

Wouldn't you know the girl turns out to be Destinee. Why am I not surprised? She's determined to get girls in the game.

To make things worse, Destinee and Asher are calling the game between the Atwater Pikes and the Red Tigers. We can't look bad—not in front of her.

Kenneth is furious. Refuses to pitch. "You can play or sit out," says David. "It's your choice."

After thinking it over, Kenneth goes to the mound. The Red Tigers have a good pitcher, too. His name is Ray Wang, and he was an all-star player last year.

We only play five innings in practice games, so we're in the bottom of the fifth. No outs. The score is 2-1 in the Tigers' favor.

I'm at bat. Ray steps up to the mound. He hurls a ball by me so fast, all I see is smoke. "Strike," Asher calls. The next two pitches are balls. The fourth pitch is coming so fast that when I decide to swing, it's in the catcher's glove. The count is two and two. I swing at the next pitch and I'm out.

Kenneth hits a ground ball right past the shortstop—good for a single. Great play. Wow.

String's up next. He slams the first pitch into center field. Kenneth advances to second and String is at first. One out. We've got a good chance at a comeback.

With the tying run at second and the winning run at first, Deshawn hits a pop fly to left field and the players on base advance. Two outs. Next up is Taylor. He connects with a ball that zips toward third base. The third baseman lunges for it, but it pops out of his glove and rolls away. Lincoln signals for Kenneth to stay put. But he ignores Lincoln and makes a dash for home plate. He slides into home, but he's tagged at the same time.

"Out!" shouts Destinee.

"No way," Kenneth yells, stomping his foot. "You know I was safe, Snoot Face. I was safe all day long."

Suddenly I'm beside Kenneth yelling, too. "He was safe, Bat Brain, and you know it!"

"You were out," Destinee screams back.

In disputes like this, it's the counselor ump who settles it. So everybody looks to David. "Sorry we don't have instant replay, but Destinee's right. You're out, Kenneth."

Kenneth doesn't accept it even then. "I was safe," he mumbles, walking to the sidelines. "I hate Destinee Tate," he says. Me too!

The dinner bell rings. It's time to clean up for dinner, but I'm not very hungry.

6:45 P.M.

After we eat, Lincoln asks me to help him sort the mail for delivery.

"What do you think about Destinee's

call this afternoon?" Lincoln asks.

"Destinee lost the game for us. I hate Destinee Tate."

"Kenneth was out," Lincoln says in his quiet way. "He didn't have to run. Why do you think he did?"

"Spare was up at bat next," I explain. "And he can't hit a beach ball. Kenneth was trying to score—tie the game so we might have a chance of winning."

Lincoln hands me a letter. It's from Mama. I'd know her writing anywhere. I tuck the letter in my pocket to read later.

"Baseball is a team sport," Lincoln is saying. "As a player on a team, you have to think about what's good for the whole team—not just yourself."

I've never had a coach before. We play in the park or at recess. And we make up the rules as we go along. I know a lot of stats. But nobody has ever talked to me about how to play the game.

"Kenneth made the decision to run because he didn't trust his teammates. He didn't listen to his coach. And when he failed, he chose to yell at the umpire. Getting all bent out of shape, calling people names, does not change the fact that he was out."

Everything is quiet for a long while. We sort more mail. Taylor got a letter. Deshawn got two.

Then Lincoln asks me why I play baseball.

"'Cause it's fun, and I enjoy it."

Lincoln puts rubber bands around each stack of letters.

"Try not to forget that. Okay?"

10:00 P.M.

It's been a long day. We're all ready for bed. Tub is complaining that he misses his television. Deshawn is showing pictures of his baby sister to anyone who'll look. All String can talk about is his mother's meat loaf and "smashed" potatoes—as he calls them. Horace misses his pillow. Taylor misses his dog. And I have to admit that I'm missing home right now myself.

Kenneth is the only one who's happy.

"Got a letter from Mom," he says. "Dad's coming for the all-star game. He's actually taking off from work to come see me."

I'm happy for him. "You're sure to make the team," I say. Kenneth smiles. He wants to be with his father more than anything. So I'm glad Mr. Peck is coming.

It will be good to see Daddy, Mama, and even Leesie. I re-read Mama's letter for the third time. The whole family is driving up for Family Weekend on Saturday and Sunday. After the all-star game on Sunday, camp is officially over. We can go home on the bus or with our families.

Mama says Leesie's got a job at an ice cream store, and she and Prince Creep have broken up. There is justice in this world.

Mama is rehearsing for an audition with the local symphony orchestra coming up in August. And Daddy is busier than ever. He wrote a note at the bottom of the letter saying there's a big fish just waiting for us to catch. Sounds good to me.

"Everything fine at home?" Lincoln asks.

"Leesie's coming for Family Weekend," I say, knowing that's what he really wants to hear. Lincoln just grins. If he knew Leesie like I do, he'd rather take on the headless Frenchman.

Monday, June 15, 9:30 A.M.

We're at the arts and crafts center putting the final touches on our team T-shirts. We're painting *The Atwater Pikes* on the front in silver block letters. On the back we're putting our names and numbers. I'm #20.

Asher is still excited about calling that game with Destinee. "She's cool. Smart, too," he says. "Are you going to sign her petition?"

Before I can say anything, Kenneth chimes in again. "Any boy who signs that petition is a wuss," he says. "He doesn't deserve to hold a bat on the same team with real players."

"I'm signing it," says Asher. "And I think Juno will put a paw print on it, too."

String steps right up. "I'm signing," he says, never raising his voice. "What about you, Miami?"

"I'm with Kenneth," I say. "I wouldn't sign Destinee Tate's petition in a million years."

Somebody groans. Somebody else snickers. String just shakes his head.

10:50 A.M.

We're practicing our hitting. Kenneth is sitting on the sidelines. I'm reminding Spare to keep his eye on the ball.

"Miami, why are you going along with

Kenneth?" String asks. "You know he's wrong."

"What I know is that Destinee is my main enemy," I say. "She's always trying to run things. Take charge."

String shakes his head. "You just don't get it sometimes. It's not about Destinee. It's about what's fair."

"Straight up," says Deshawn.

"There should just be one all-star team with the best players—both girls and boys," says Tub. "Look at the girls' stats, man. Some of them are as good as us."

"Destinee can't be all that good. She just started playing this spring," I say.

"The girl is a natural," says Jamaka. "She can hit, run, do it all. And she's getting better every day. Check out her numbers."

"I'm not signing that stupid petition, no matter what you think!"

"'Cause Kenneth says so?" Deshawn asks.

"No, because I say so!" My voice echoes across the field. "I knew she was going to be trouble. I knew it. I hate that Destinee Tate."

"Way to go," says Kenneth from the sidelines.

"SHUT UP!" I shout.

6
The Right to Be Wrong

Tuesday, June 16, 6:30 P.M.

We-the-People, Taylor, String, Asher, and I signed up for the archaeological dig. We spent the day looking at fossils and rocks that are millions of years old. Boy, was it kicking! We even got to see the footprint of a real dinosaur.

We're back now. And all the word is that Destinee and the girls are going to present the petition to Sandy.

Kenneth has other ideas. He's waiting for Destinee at the main lodge door. He blocks her way. "Give me that petition," he says, smirking.

I don't like what Kenneth is doing, even though it's Destinee Tate. And I hate that girl.

Destinee glares at him. Suddenly, Kenneth pushes her and grabs her arm. Her face twists in pain. "The petition," he insists.

Then I realize Kenneth hates, *hates* Destinee. I have to do something. But Kenneth is so much bigger than me.

He reaches for the papers. In a quick move, Destinee sidesteps him and twists Kenneth's pointer finger backwards. What a play.

Now it is Kenneth's turn to struggle in pain. "Oh, please, please. I'm sorry," he whines.

Destinee doesn't let go but takes the pressure off—just a little.

"Repeat after me?" Destinee's got him on his knees. "I am a wanna-be thug. Say it?"

"I am a wanna-be thug."

Man! I can't believe he said it. Wow!

"No more trouble. Okay?" She lets go of his finger.

Kenneth is so angry. He reaches for a rock to throw at Destinee. But I step in.

"Drop the rock, creep," I say. What's wrong with this picture? Me. Me defending Destinee Tate. "She beat you fair and square, Kenneth. Accept it."

"I thought you hated Destinee Tate."

"I do, but I don't like you at all," I tell him.

For the first time, he doesn't look all that big to me. He's a sad boy. Not tough. Not smart. Not at all like my buddy String.

"I won't play on a team with girls," he shouts.

"Who cares?"

Once we get inside, Destinee takes me to the side. "Hey, thanks, Miami. Why did you help me?" she asks.

"The way I figure," I say, "you've got a right to be wrong without somebody in your face. And that's the only reason why I'm signing this petition."

Destinee smiles as I scribble my name across the bottom of the page. "Anything you say, Miami."

I call after her, "Where'd you learn that finger thing?"

"My dad. He used to be a marine."

Wednesday, June 17, 1:00 P.M.

Sandy's got the petition.

At lunch he announces that this year's Atwater all-star team will include both boys and girls. "This camp experience is yours. So my staff and I have decided that if this is what you want, this is the way it will be."

Some of the guys are grumbling at first, but then the girls begin beating on the table.

The place goes wild. Everybody is chanting, "San-dy, San-dy, San-dy." Sandy is ah-right.

I look around at Kenneth. He looks tore-down. Slammed!

Then Sandy passes out the ballots for us to vote on the Atwater all-star team. Everybody gets to choose twenty players and three camper umpires. But this year we get to choose both girls and boys.

I choose myself, of course. Then I check off String and all the guys that I think are good players.

I'm down to two choices.

I can vote for Kenneth, but Lincoln says baseball is a team sport, played for fun. I don't vote for Kenneth. I can also vote for Destinee. I have to give it to her. She stood up for what she thought was right. That's more than I did with Kenneth. She's earned the right to play. So I quickly vote for her and turn in my ballot before I change my mind. Thank goodness for secret ballots.

7:00 P.M.

As always the campers gather to lower the flag and then go to our evening program. This evening we go back to the main lodge to hear the results of the bal-loting.

After blowing into the mike, Sandy rais-es his hand to get our attention. "I am pleased to announce this year's head coach for the all-star team will be Lincoln Thomas," he says, sounding like a circus master.

"Way to go, Lincoln!"

Then Sandy gives Lincoln the mike and he begins calling the names of the all-star team.

I'm sitting very still, listening. Please. Please let me make it. Lincoln rattles on and on. I hear everybody cheer when String's name is called.

When Destinee's name is called, Sandy takes the mike. "This is the player who decided that Camp Atwater needed to come into the twenty-first century," he says, smiling. Then his face becomes serious. "I lost sight for a moment of what this camp is about. It's about fair play and having fun. Thank you, Destinee, for reminding me. And congratulations."

Lots more cheering. I'm so nervous. Asher leans over and whispers, "Don't worry, you'll make it."

Lincoln has called almost fifteen names when I hear him say, "Miami Jackson." I've made it. Yes! High-fives are flying from all around.

"This last person you selected was a complete surprise to me," says Lincoln. "I'm proud to announce that you selected Asher to be one of the all-star team umpires."

The place goes wild again. Everybody's

standing up cheering and applauding.

Asher is truly surprised. "How? I wasn't even on the ballot."

"I wrote your name in," I say. I was thinking I was the only one who did.

"I wrote your name in, too," says String.

"Me too," say Tub and Horace.

I guess everybody had the same idea. Fifteen boys and five girls will take the field against the Lazy B team. No girls for them. They'll only be bringing their boys' team this year. Lincoln believes we can beat them. I believe it, too.

Kenneth? Well, he didn't make the team. All that talent gone to waste. But he's the one who said he wouldn't play on a team with girls. He got his wish.

7
Family and Friends

The all-star players have been practicing together for two days. We're as ready as we'll ever be.

Deshawn's folks are the first parents to arrive for Family Weekend. They come in right after breakfast. Deshawn is glad to see his baby sister. He lets me hold her. Boy, is she cute with two teeth on the bottom.

A lot of parents can't make it because they live too far away. But family members who live close by come to see their nephews, nieces, cousins—even brothers and sisters. Jamaka's brother from Madison drove over to be with him.

Kenneth's mother is here. But not his father. At the last minute he had a business meeting to attend. Kenneth looks madder and meaner than ever before.

All week he's been sulking. Nobody's really surprised to learn that Kenneth is leaving early—this afternoon. Not even staying for the big game.

I stop by to say good-bye. "Sorry the way things went down," I say.

Kenneth shrugs. "Who cares? Did you know my dad played for Atlanta in the early '90s?"

I just put two and two together. Atlanta. Peck. "Joey Peck is your dad? He was one of the best relief pitchers in the game."

"Yep," says Kenneth. "That's him."

"You are so lucky to have Joey Peck as your father."

Kenneth laughs, but his eyes aren't laughing. He tosses his bag over his shoulder. "Gotta go," he says. And like that, he's gone.

1:00 P.M.

String's folks are here. Mr. and Mrs. Tate arrive not long after them.

I'm wondering if Mama and Daddy will ever get here when they come driving up. I introduce my family to my friends—Taylor, Spare, Deshawn, Tub, and all the rest. They like Asher and Juno right away. Daddy is amazed that Asher is blind yet he can call a game.

Mama is proud of me making the all-stars. "Are you playing guard?" she asks.

"Mama!"

"What?"

She's just teasing. She knows there are no guards in baseball.

And Lincoln finally gets to meet Leesie. I haven't seen her blush like this since her last boyfriend, Prince Creep, came on the scene. Lincoln asks her to go to the bonfire with him. She says yes. So now she's at the guest lodge trying to get glamorous.

2:30 P.M.

Meanwhile the all-star team is gathering for the final practice for the big game tomorrow.

Daddy walks down to one of the fields to toss a few balls with me. "I was a bit worried about you being away from home by yourself," he says. "But you seem to have done very well on your own." Daddy sounds proud.

"I know you're busy," I tell him. "I'm glad you took time to come up here—to come see me play."

"You know you can count on me," he says. That's what makes it okay with us.

I tell Daddy about Kenneth. "I was impressed with Kenneth because he was bigger and stronger and could play well. But that didn't make him a good friend. I've got some really good friends. And String is the best of them all."

"You can tell a lot about a person by the company he or she keeps. It seems you have made good choices."

Choices. That's what Camp Atwater has been about. "Lincoln says baseball is a game of choices. I won't ever forget that."

Then I tell him about Destinee and how I chose to vote for her—even though she's my archenemy. "You should have seen that finger twist thing she did with Kenneth. It was awesome."

Daddy burns a fastball into my glove. "Call the fire department," he says, laughing. "This takes me back to when I was your age." Daddy's on a roll. "But this is much nicer than the camp I attended." He goes on forever, talking about camp life in the 1970s—a long, long time ago.

"We had to sleep in a tent. No electricity. There were no nice lodges like you've got here. This is a resort by comparison."

"And you had to go fetch your own water without shoes, right?" I say, imitating my grandfathers telling about when they were boys.

"Right…" Daddy stops and smiles. He asks, "Am I sounding like Papa Michael?"

"And Grandpa Andrew, too," I answer, laughing.

"They walked ten miles to school…"

"In the snow…" I add.

Then we both say, "Uphill both ways."

8:00 P.M.

The bonfire and barbecue for Camp Atwater and the Lazy B Camp is kicking. Cookie has laid out a spread. Tub has eaten so many ribs I think he is going to start oinking.

We dance and sing, doing everything from square dancing to hip-hop. The adults love the oldies-but-goodies songs. They look so funny doing all those dances from the '70s.

I don't think Lincoln has left Leesie's side once. She doesn't seem to mind. Nothing but teeth showing all night.

String and I check out the Lazy B players. They look good and they sure eat a lot. I'm so busy eyeballing them, I run into Destinee at the dessert table.

"What's up, Frog Lips?" she says, right in front of a Lazy B player.

I've been good all week. No more Mr. Nice Guy. "Why don't you flip *your* lips over your head and swallow yourself?" I say.

"Now, now," she answers, clicking her tongue. "We're teammates." And she waves me off like a worrisome gnat or something.

"I hate Destinee Tate," I growl.

String just shakes his head.

8
It's All Atwater

Sunday, June 21, Noon

Game time.

Asher and one of the umps from Lazy B will call the first three innings at the plate with David. Then a new set will take over for three more innings with a counselor from Lazy B, and a final set of umps for the last three innings.

We're home so we take the field first. I'm happy at first base. String is catching. Destinee is at third base. Ray Wang is pitching for us.

"Batter up!"

Ray retires the first three Lazy B players one, two, three—a strikeout, an easy out at first base, and a pop fly. We don't do any better. I strike out. Forever a sucker for fastballs. I just don't see them.

Second inning, third inning. Asher does a wonderful job. Everybody gives him a standing ovation when Juno leads him off the field.

Fourth inning, fifth inning. Couple of threats but nothing materializes for us or for them. Lincoln is giving us pep talks from the sidelines. Encouraging us to hang in there. We're trying, that's for sure.

Then, during the top of the seventh inning, a Lazy B player hits a home run with one player on. As he passes me at first base, he laughs, saying, "We're going to mash you like a bunch of potatoes." Suddenly the score is 2-0, Lazy B.

Lincoln won't let us lose our spirits. "Hang in there," he says. "Hustle, hustle!"

It's the bottom of the eighth. I hit a line drive into left field and get to first. The next batter bunts. She's thrown out at first base, but I advance to second. The next player hits a line drive right down the third-base line. Lincoln signals me to hang at second and the hitter makes it to first.

Then Destinee's up. She hits a sacrifice fly deep into center field. As soon as it's caught, I tag up and dash for third. Should I keep going?

Tagging third base, I take a quick look at Lincoln. He waves me home. But home base looks a mile away. It's not about me, I tell myself. It's what's good for the team. I lower my head and kick for home.

The catcher is poised to get the ball. I

have to make it. I'm running as hard as I can. Then I forget about everything and dive for the base. As my fingers touch the pad, I hear the magic word. "Safe!"

The crowd roars. I hear Daddy's voice, saying, "That's my son!" Even Leesie is jumping up and down. There is so much hand slapping, my palms are sore.

"Way to go, Miami," says Destinee. And before I know it Destinee and I are high-fiving each other. For the team, I tell myself. For the team.

But we've got to get back in the game. Lazy B sends in another pitcher and he strikes out our next batter, leaving a player stranded on third. But at least the score is 2-1 going into the ninth.

We're able to keep them from scoring. So, it's the bottom of the ninth.

Two of our players get on with a walk and a dropped fly. String's at bat. He takes a strike and two balls. The next pitch comes like a birthday gift. It floats up to the plate and hangs there for him to hit it all the way out of the field. He clears the bases and the game is over 4-2 in our favor. It's all Atwater!

Atwater campers crowd out onto the field. Sandy is so excited he's leaping like a wild deer. He lifts String up on his shoulders. Suddenly I feel myself being lifted off my feet. I look to my right and Destinee is up there, too. Oh, well. I'm too happy to worry about a thing. Right now I don't even hate Destinee Tate—as much.

9
Chance Encounter

Two months later

Where did the summer go? It seems like yesterday we were getting out of school and on our way to Camp Atwater. Now school is about to start.

After camp, summer seemed to zip by like the Road Runner. String and I hear from Asher through e-mail at least once a week. I haven't heard from Kenneth. But I did read in the paper that his father signed a big deal with a huge sports complex that is being built in Knoxville. I wonder about Kenneth sometimes.

Dad is right, I'll never forget the friends

and the good times I had at Atwater. Can't wait to go next year. But for now, school's about to start.

Leesie is beginning her senior year at Kirkland High. She's been shopping for clothes all week. "I can't be a role model to the little Freshies by wearing just anything," she says.

But when Mama sees what Leesie's bought, she shakes her head. "You didn't pay money for that, did you?"

"Where's the rest of that skimpy little outfit?" says Daddy.

Leesie, the Queen of Drama, runs to her room, whining, "You don't understand anything!"

Lincoln stopped by to see Leesie on his way back to college. It was good seeing him. In fact, Lincoln is the first guy who's come to visit Leesie that Daddy seems to like. I still don't get what Lincoln sees in her. Daddy says I will one day.

Mama's in the local orchestra, playing first chair oboe. And getting ready for school to start again herself. I hope she gets afternoon classes so our mornings will go smoother. Daddy's finished his project and is bidding on another job.

The rest of our summer was a bunch of choices. Like Lincoln said on the first day of camp, we could choose to have fun or choose to be bored. String and I went for the fun.

We played baseball a lot. We even got to a couple Cardinals games. Destinee spent most of the summer with her grandparents in Boston. String says she's coming home Sunday—like I care.

We both got certificates for reading over twenty books in the summer reading program at the library. We also got swimming cards for joining the swim program at the Y. It's been a good summer.

1:30 P.M.

I'm supposed to be meeting String at the discount store to buy our school supplies.

I park and lock my bicycle by the door, grab a cart, and begin to roll it into the store. Without warning, this lady comes from out of the twilight zone and crashes into me with her cart. Wham!

I slide to the floor. She drops her purse and her glasses almost flop off her face.

"Excuse me," I say. "I'm sorry. My fault."

"A young person with some manners," she says, sounding surprised. "You're an endangered species, young man. Tell me, what is your name?"

"Miami Jackson."

"My class list shows that a Michael Andrew Jackson will be coming to my fourth-grade class at Turner. Are you by any chance that young man?"

I'm thinking, please don't let this be true. Please. I was signed up to be with Mrs. O'Shay. "Did you say fourth grade?"

"Yes. Mrs. O'Shay is moving away. And I've been given the fourth-grade class."

I swallow. "Yes, ma'am. Then I guess I am the Michael Andrew on your list. But most people call me Miami."

"Not me, young man. I don't approve of nicknames. You are Michael Andrew and

I'm Miss Amerita Spraggins." She extends her hand.

It would be too rude for me not to shake it, so I do. "See you in a few days," she says. "Ready to learn, I trust. Good day." And she swishes away.

"Who was that?" String asks, coming up behind me.

"Christopher Lee Tyler," I say, calling String by his full name. "You don't want to know."

Authors' Note

Many readers ask if String and Destinee are real kids. All of our characters are fictional, but they are based on real kids in our lives. In this story, Asher is based on a boy named John. We met John at a YMCA camp nearly twenty years ago. He had lost his sight at an early age, but he had an unusual gift.

By standing behind a catcher, John could call balls and strikes with remarkable accuracy. Though it seems unbelievable, he had a sharper sense of hearing than most people. He could tell, by listening to where and how a pitch was caught, what the call should be. If the ball dropped away from the batter, it was a "low, outside ball." When John felt the catcher reach up and in, he called a "high, inside ball." And when the ball zinged right over the plate, his call was usually, "Strike!"

There was no magic about it. John practiced a lot. He was very self-confident. And he loved the game of baseball.